characters created by lauren child

Charlie is
broken!

Grosset & Dunlap

Charlie and Lola™

Text based on the script written by Bridget Hurst   Illustrations from the TV animation   Produced by Tiger Aspect

GROSSET & DUNLAP
Published by the Penguin Group
Penguin Group (USA) Inc., 375 Hudson Street, New York, New York 10014, USA
Penguin Group (Canada), 90 Eglinton Avenue East, Suite 700, Toronto, Ontario M4P 2Y3, Canada
(a division of Pearson Penguin Canada Inc.)
Penguin Books Ltd., 80 Strand, London WC2R 0RL, England
Penguin Group Ireland, 25 St. Stephen's Green, Dublin 2, Ireland
(a division of Penguin Books Ltd.)
Penguin Group (Australia), 250 Camberwell Road, Camberwell, Victoria 3124, Australia
(a division of Pearson Australia Group Pty. Ltd.)
Penguin Books India Pvt. Ltd., 11 Community Centre, Panchsheel Park, New Delhi—110 017, India
Penguin Group (NZ), 67 Apollo Drive, Rosedale, North Shore 0632, New Zealand
(a division of Pearson New Zealand Ltd.)
Penguin Books (South Africa) (Pty.) Ltd., 24 Sturdee Avenue,
Rosebank, Johannesburg 2196, South Africa

Penguin Books Ltd., Registered Offices: 80 Strand, London WC2R 0RL, England

Library of Congress Cataloging-in-Publication Data is available.

ISBN 978-0-448-45237-1   10 9 8

I have this little sister, Lola.
She is small and very funny.
Today we are busy practicing
for a special CIRCUS show.

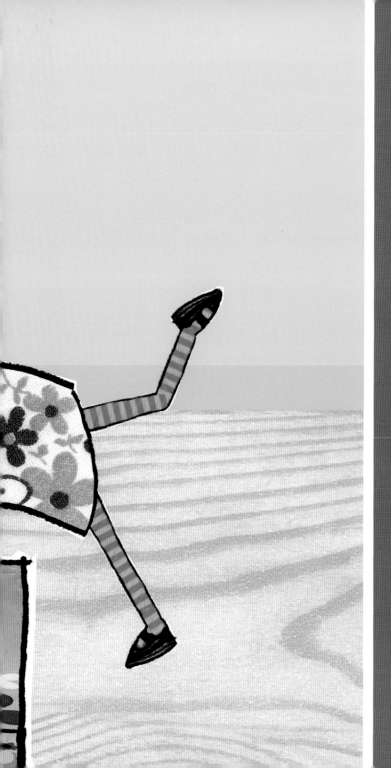

Lola is trying
    to do **somersaults.**

She says,
"It's not working, Charlie.
    You have to push me."

Lola says, "Tada!"

And I cheer.

Then Lola says,
"But I must be able
          to do a somersault
all on my own!"

At the park,
Lola and Lotta
        practice **somersaults**.
They can nearly do them
                all on their own.
        But not quite.

So I say,
        "Maybe you should
practice **bowing** instead."

        And Lola says,
"That's a good idea!"

Then Marv says,
                "Come on, Charlie.
        Let's play soccer!"

Lola and Lotta
practice taking **bows**
while Marv and I
play soccer.

But then I fall over
and **hurt** my arm.

"Ouch!"

It really, really **hurts**.

Dad takes me
     to the hospital.

When I get home,
Lola asks,
     "Charlie, why is
your arm white
     and GINORMOUS?"

And I say,
"That's my cast, Lola.
     It protects my arm
until it's all better."

Then Lola says,
     "I hope you will
be better for our
     circus show."

Later, Lola says,
"Aren't you hungry?"

And I say,
"No, I'm thinking
        of all the things
I can't do because
        my arm's **broken**.

I won't be able to
play with my dinosaurs or
        get dressed by myself.
And I don't think
        I'll be able to do
the **circus** show, either."

That night,
    Lola can't sleep . . .

"I'm a bit slightly scared.
    Charlie isn't Charlie
anymore.
        He is broken.

And when you
        are broken,
    you have to be very
extremely careful.
        And you might
need a nurse
        to help you."

The next day,
          Lola says,
"I brought you
          some pink milk, Charlie,
to make you better.

"And eating cereal
          will make you
much more better.

"I can even **help** you
brush your teeth . . .

"And I know a way
        you can still be in
our **Circus** show."

I say,
        "But Lola,
I just want to stay
        completely still.
        And that's not good
for the show."

And Lola says,
        "It is! It is very
        completely good!"

At our **circus** show,
Lola says,
"Look how Charlie
is more stiller than
the stillest thing
in the whole, wide
universe and world!

And look!
Even when I do
my **somersaults**,
he will not move!"

Lola does
a **somersault**
          all by herself.

She says,
     "Tada!"

Then she says,
     "Oh! Did I do that
all on my own?"

     I laugh.

     And Lola says,
"Oh! He moved!
          See everyone,
Charlie is **better**!"

Then Lola looks at my cast
and says, "Well, *nearly* better!"